Robert

and the
Stolen Bike

Also by Barbara Seuling

Oh No, It's Robert

Robert and the Attack of the Giant Tarantula

Robert and the Snake Escape

Robert and the Great Pepperoni

Robert and the Sneaker Snobs

Robert and the Instant Millionaire *Show*

Robert and the Three Wishes

Robert and the Hairy Disaster

Robert and the Scariest Night

Robert and the Clickety-clackety Teeth

Robert and the Troublesome Tuba

Robert and the Embarrassing Secret

Robert and the Class President

Robert and the World's Worst Wristwatch

Robert and the Chocolate Worms

Robert and the Three Star Rotten Day

Robert and the Computer Hogs

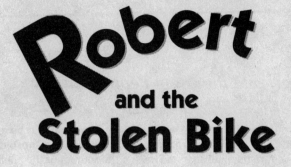

Robert
and the
Stolen Bike

by Barbara Seuling
Illustrated by Paul Brewer

A
LITTLE APPLE
PAPERBACK

SCHOLASTIC INC.
New York Toronto London Auckland Sydney
Mexico City New Delhi Hong Kong Buenos Aires

No part of this publication may be reproduced in whole or in part, or stored in a retrieval system, or transmitted in any form or by any means, electronic, mechanical, photocopying, recording, or otherwise, without written permission of the publisher. For information regarding permission, write to Carus Publishing Company, 315 Fifth Street, Peru, Illinois 61354.

ISBN 0-439-58750-6

Text copyright © 2005 by Barbara Seuling.
Illustrations copyright © 2005 by Paul Brewer.

All rights reserved. Published by Scholastic Inc., 557 Broadway, New York, NY 10012, by arrangement with Carus Publishing Company. SCHOLASTIC and associated logos are trademarks and/or registered trademarks of Scholastic Inc.

12 11 10 9 8 7 6 5 4 3 2   6 7 8 9 10/0

Printed in the U.S.A.   40
First Scholastic printing, May 2005

for Taylor Jansen
—B. S.

for Becki, Kevin, Elliot, and Andy Krull
—P. B.

Contents

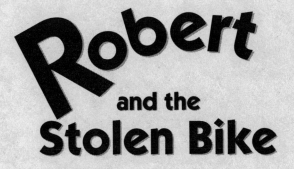

The New Girl

Mrs. Bernthal sat on a high stool with a book open in her hands. Every afternoon, she read to the class. They were in the middle of *The Tale of Despereaux* by Kate DeCamillo.

Robert wrapped his feet around the legs of his chair and listened to Mrs. Bernthal's voice.

"*. . . no one noticed as Roscuro crawled up a table leg and onto the table, and from there flung himself onto the lowest branch of the chandelier. . . . Hanging by one paw he*

swung back and forth, admiring the specta-
cle below him; the smells of the food, the
sound of the music. . . ."

A knock on the door interrupted Mrs.
Bernthal. Mr. Lipkin, the principal, opened
the door and peered in. "May we come in?"
he asked.

"Of course, Mr. Lipkin," said Mrs.
Bernthal. "Children, what do you say?"

"Good afternoon, Mr. Lipkin," they said
in unison.

"Thank you, children," said Mr. Lipkin.
Next to him was a blond-haired girl in a
checked shirt.

"This is Taylor Jerome," Mr. Lipkin
continued. "Taylor just moved into the
neighborhood, and is going to join your
class."

Mrs. Bernthal smiled at Taylor.

Mr. Lipkin whispered something to Mrs.
Bernthal. She nodded as he left.

Mrs. Bernthal looked directly at Taylor. "We're happy to have you in our class, Taylor. You will sit at Table Four," she said, taking her over to the table where Robert and Paul and Vanessa sat. "This will be your seat." Taylor sat down.

"Robert and Paul and Vanessa, will you help Taylor if she has any questions about what we're working on?" All three of them nodded.

"Class," Mrs. Bernthal continued, "Taylor is hearing impaired. She is learning sign language, but she reads lips. So when you speak, be sure you are facing her."

Mrs. Bernthal picked up the book to continue their story. Robert wanted to hear what happened next, but at the same time, he was fascinated by Taylor. Could she hear anything? Could she really understand the story by reading Mrs. Bernthal's lips? Should they tell her what they were reading? He tried to get her attention, but Taylor never took her eyes off Mrs. Bernthal.

Before he knew it, the bell rang and the class was dismissed. Robert never did hear what happened in the story. He'd have to ask Paul Felcher, his best friend.

"Hey, Paul!" he shouted, running out of the school building. Paul was already outside, waiting for him.

"You want to come over?" Robert asked as they started their walk home. They almost never took the school bus on nice days, and they almost always did their homework together.

"Yeah," answered Paul. "I'll call my mom from your house."

"So what happened to that mouse that was hanging from the chandelier?" Robert asked.

"He fell. Into the queen's soup."

5

"Get out of here!"

"No, really!" said Paul.

"And what happened then?"

"The bell rang."

"Oh." Robert was glad he hadn't missed too much.

"We need to practice our lines," Robert said. Mrs. Bernthal had them putting on a play called *The Secret of the Pirate King*. Everyone in the class was a pirate or a sailor. Robert and Paul were Dirty Pete and Greenteeth, two of the pirate band.

"You think the new girl will be in the play?" asked Robert.

"Sure. Everyone is in it. Why?"

"She's deaf."

"But Mrs. Bernthal said she can read lips."

"So we all have to face her when we say our lines?"

"I guess," said Paul.

Robert wondered how that would work. They reached his house while he was still thinking about it.

Huckleberry met them at the door, his tail wagging.

"Hi, boy," said Robert, scratching behind the big Lab's yellow ears.

After Paul called his mom, they went upstairs to Robert's room. Huckleberry followed them and jumped up on Robert's bed. Robert and Paul dropped their backpacks there, too. Then they sat in the beanbag chair. That's where they did their best thinking. The trouble was, they were supposed to be thinking about the play, but all Robert could think about was the new girl.

Pirates and Sailors

The next day, Robert waited until Taylor looked his way before he said "Hi," and he raised his hand in a little wave, too. He wondered if that was like sign language. Taylor smiled and gave a little wave back.

It was time to rehearse their parts for the play. Mrs. Bernthal said they would have to work on their set if they were going to have the play ready in two weeks.

"Who would like to paint our set?" she asked, turning to Paul automatically. Paul was the best artist in the class. He raised his hand.

"And who would like to help Paul?" Mrs. Bernthal asked. Lots of hands went up, including Robert's. "Okay," said Mrs. Bernthal, "Lester . . . Robert . . . Lucy . . . Oh! and Taylor."

After the set painters were appointed, Mrs. Bernthal gave everyone permission to move around so they could rehearse their lines for the play together.

"Recite your lines to one another before you get up in front of the class to try them." She looked at Robert. "Robert, will you work with Taylor, please? I gave her the part of a sailor, the lookout, and she has two lines to speak. She will have to memorize them and practice them with you. Be sure she understands what she must do."

Robert looked at Taylor. She had understood, because she whirled around in her chair to look at him.

"Okay," he said.

Had he faced Taylor when he said that? Did she read his lips? He said it again, just to be sure. "OKAY."

He realized immediately that it was too loud. Kids at nearby tables stopped what they were doing to turn and look at him.

Robert and Paul exchanged seats so Robert could sit across from Taylor.

"You go first," he said, pointing to the pages of the script.

Taylor looked at the pages in front of her. She stared for a minute, then looked up.

"Ahoy!" she shouted. "There's a ship on the horizon!"

Robert was surprised at what he heard. The last words sounded thick, like they were covered with honey, and had a hard time coming out.

"That was good," he said. But Taylor's shoulders sagged.

Why didn't anyone tell him Taylor's voice would sound—different? Now they were both embarrassed. It hadn't been so bad, but no one had told him what to expect. He could have been a lot cooler about it.

"I'll do mine," Robert said, pushing his pages aside and standing up. He had memorized his lines. He had just two short sentences to say. He pretended to have a sword in his hand and held it high. He looked straight at Taylor. "I'm Dirty Pete with the smelly feet!" he cried. "Get out of me way!"

For a moment, it was totally quiet. Then everyone at Table Four cracked up. Even Taylor. Robert was relieved. His lines had never sounded so funny before.

Later, in the cafeteria, Robert and Paul were standing in line to get their milk when Robert noticed Taylor sitting alone at a table. A few girls were at the same table, but they were talking among themselves, and Taylor was sitting apart from them.

"Look," said Robert.

Paul turned to look. "What?" he asked.

"Taylor. The deaf girl. She's sitting by herself."

Paul nodded. "Want to sit with her?"

"Maybe." Robert wasn't sure. What would they say? What if Taylor sounded funny again, and it showed on his face?

"Yeah, okay," said Paul.

They got their milk and walked over to the table where Taylor sat. She looked up.

The look on her face told Robert they had done the right thing.

"Hi," he said. "I'm Dirty Pete with the smelly feet. Can we sit here?"

Taylor smiled. She looked grateful.

Paul slid in next to Robert. "Hi," he said. "Greenteeth here."

Taylor smiled. "Hi," she said. It didn't come out funny. It sounded perfectly okay.

They opened their lunches and started eating.

"What have you got?" asked Robert.

Taylor looked at her sandwich. "Peanut butter," she said. Robert heard a kind of thick sound, but he could understand her perfectly. "And an apple." She held up the apple.

"I have baloney," said Robert. He opened his sandwich and ate the baloney off the top, leaving the bread. "Oh, and chocolate-covered jelly cookies."

"Salami," said Paul, showing his sandwich. "And a brownie."

This wasn't hard at all. Robert felt himself relaxing as they ate their sandwiches and sipped their milk noisily through their straws.

Gone

"Too bad Lester and Lucy couldn't make it this afternoon," said Paul, locking his bike to the bike rack outside the library.

"And Taylor," Robert reminded him, leaning his bike against the rack. "Don't forget she's a part of the team."

"Right," said Paul. "I'm still getting used to having a new kid in class."

"I know," said Robert. He was glad Paul said "a new kid." The other kids referred to Taylor as "the deaf girl." He didn't think that was too cool.

Robert wondered if he was the only one who thought about Taylor's deafness so much. He didn't feel like asking Paul about it right now, even though Paul was his best friend. He had to think about it more first.

They went into the library and found books about ships with good pictures. Paul's idea was to paint a backdrop of the sea, with cardboard waves moving up and down in front of it. Then he wanted to paint the pirate ship in three different sizes so he could start with the small one, looking like it was far away, and changing it to the bigger ones as it got closer.

"So," said Paul, "we're looking for ships from long ago, the kind that had sails."

They went through book after book, until they finally found pictures that they could use. They checked out six books and split them up so each would carry three books in his bicycle basket.

When they got outside, there was only one bike—Paul's—locked to the rack.

"My bike is gone!" cried Robert. "Somebody stole my bike!"

"Oh, no," said Paul. "Wasn't it locked?"

Robert felt stupid. "No. I just leaned it against the rack."

Paul didn't say anything, but Robert knew he must be thinking: *What a dope he is, for not locking his bicycle.*

They put all the books in Paul's basket and walked home slowly. It took them a long time, but that wasn't the part that hurt. Who would take his bicycle like that? In broad daylight? In front of the library?

When they got to Paul's corner, Robert didn't feel like stopping at Paul's to work on the play or do homework. He had to get home to tell his parents about his bike.

"I'll call you later," said Paul. He sounded so sad. Robert gave him a little wave to show he knew that Paul understood, and walked the last two blocks to his house. He hoped someone—one of his parents, at least—would be home.

"Rob, is that you?" called his mom. Huckleberry was already at his feet, waiting for his usual welcoming pat. Robert was glad to hear his mom was there.

"Yeah, it's me, Mom." He dragged himself into the kitchen, where his mom was making a cup of tea. He sat down at the table and put his head in his hands.

Huckleberry seemed to understand. He nuzzled Robert's hand.

"What's the matter, Rob?" asked his mom.

"Somebody stole my bike," he replied.

"What? Your bike? How? Where? When?" His mother sat down at the table with him. She was just as upset as he had been.

"From in front of the library. Just now. And I don't know how, Mom."

"Was it locked?"

"Um . . . no." Robert couldn't bear to look at his mother. He knew what was coming next.

"Oh, Rob. Haven't I told you a thousand times to lock up your bicycle when you're not using it?"

He nodded. He already felt stupid. He wished he didn't have to feel even more stupid.

Robert's dad walked in from the living room. "What's that? Your bike was stolen?"

Robert nodded again.

His mom got up and reached for the phone. "I'm reporting it," she said. "If someone around here has it, the police will find it."

Robert's dad raised his eyebrows. He didn't look so sure. Robert felt himself

slink down on the chair. He wished he could become invisible.

Within minutes, a police car with its lights flashing drove up the Dorfmans' driveway. Two men in uniform came to the door.

"Come in," said Mrs. Dorfman.

At another time, this might have been interesting—even exciting—but Robert felt too sad to appreciate it.

The policemen were very nice. They both asked questions, and one took down all the information in a little notebook. One of them even said Huckleberry looked like a great dog. At the very end, though, as they were leaving, one of the policemen said they would do their best, but from past experience, it was unlikely they would recover the bike.

Detective Work

It didn't take long the next morning before every kid in the class had heard about Robert's bike being stolen.

Everyone seemed upset, even Susanne Lee Rodgers, who usually looked at Robert like he was less than a worm.

"That's awful, Robert," she said.

Vanessa was really sympathetic. "I'm so sorry, Robert," she said. "I have a bike, and it's pink, but you can borrow it anytime."

Robert thought that was really sweet. He wouldn't be caught dead riding a girl's pink bike, but he knew she was trying to help.

"Thanks," he said, making an effort to smile. He didn't feel much like smiling.

Lester seemed to take it hardest of all. "I wish I had been there," he said. "Maybe it wouldn't have happened. But I had to help my dad on his route." Lester's dad was in the trash removal business.

The other kids pitched in enthusiastically.

"We can look out for it wherever we go," said Kristi Mills.

"What does it look like?" asked Emily Asher.

Paul jumped in. "I'll draw it! Then we can each make a copy to help identify the bike."

Robert was flabbergasted at all the help the kids offered. He described the bike as Paul drew it.

He described the handlebars with the blue grips and the tassels.

He described the bell that was clamped onto the handlebars.

He described the color—blue—and the white racing stripe on the frame and on the fenders.

He described the the light in the front.

He described the reflectors on the pedals and in the back.

And he described the ten-speed hand brakes.

"Wow," said Joey Rizzo. "You really know your bike, don't you?"

"Yeah," said Robert. "I love that bike." He tried hard not to cry.

Mrs. Bernthal took the bicycle picture and promised to make photocopies in the office at lunchtime.

"Let's get to work now," she called. "Tomorrow you will say your parts in front of the class, and I hope you will have them memorized," she said.

"When do we work on our costumes?" asked Kristi.

"I think you can start working on them anytime," said Mrs. Bernthal. "But don't neglect learning your lines to work on the costumes."

"Oh, great!" said Kristi. She and Emily had volunteered to be on the Costumes Committee.

"What about the props? When do we bring those in?" asked Brian Hoberman. He and Matt Blakey were the Props Committee.

"You can bring those in, and we'll just keep them here for when we need them," said Mrs. Bernthal. "If you have any other questions about what and when, ask Susanne Lee. She's the stage manager and has the schedule of when we will need everything."

"Everyone has a job," Taylor said. Robert and Paul and Vanessa all turned to look at her. She didn't say much, so when she did speak, everyone listened.

"You can be on a committee," said Vanessa. "Which one do you want to be on?"

Taylor shrugged. "It doesn't matter."

"You can help us paint the sets," said Robert.

"Yeah," said Paul.

Vanessa nodded in agreement.

Taylor smiled. "Thanks," she said.

Robert heard that heavy sound in Taylor's voice again. Why did it happen just once in a while?

Toward the end of the afternoon, Mrs. Bernthal handed out the papers with Robert's bicycle drawn and described.

"We'll keep our eyes open," said Joey.

"Yeah, true detectives," said Matt Blakey.

Robert felt a little bit better knowing the kids were so willing to help him find his bike, but he couldn't forget what that policeman had said: It was unlikely they would ever recover the bike.

Google™

"Can I look something up on the computer?" Robert asked. He and Paul were at Paul's house, doing their homework in Paul's room.

"Sure," said Paul. "What are you looking for?"

"You'll think I'm weird," Robert said.

"But you are weird," said Paul.

"Seriously," said Robert. "I need to find out something, and I don't want you to laugh."

"Okay, I won't laugh." Paul covered his mouth to keep from laughing.

28

"You're not being serious," said Robert, beginning to laugh himself.

"Well, tell me then, since I'm already laughing."

"I want to find out something about deafness."

Afer they got the laughing out of their systems, they settled down again. Paul went over to the computer and clicked on to the search screen.

"Okay, just type in your question," he said, getting up to give Robert the chair.

Robert sat down. He thought. Then he typed: CAN YOU TELL ME ABOUT DEAFNESS?

A list of items came back. Robert didn't know where to begin. He was about to get up when Paul came over again.

"What's the matter?"

"There's just too much. I don't know what to pick."

"Okay." Paul started over again and typed in DEAFNESS.

A long list of items came up again, but this time Robert read a couple that sounded good. He clicked on an information center. It was all about programs for the deaf and doctors who worked with deaf people.

He tried again. This one was titled, "Answers to Your Questions About Deafness." It was interesting, and he learned that Thomas Edison, who invented the lightbulb, was deaf. But it didn't answer his question.

What *was* his question? Did he even know? Yeah. He wanted to know why Taylor sounded funny sometimes.

"Did you find what you're looking for?" asked Paul after a few minutes.

"No."

"Sometimes you have to try again, using different words."

Robert knew he had to have "deaf" in there, but he really wanted to know about how deaf people speak. He typed in DEAF SPEECH.

Wow! This looked more like it. There was a lot about speech therapy, and sounds, and . . .

There it was! "Listen to this!" he shouted.

"What?" said Paul.

"Deaf people have the hardest time with *sh, ch,* and *th* sounds. Maybe that's it!"

Paul looked confused. Robert kept babbling. "I think that's it! When Taylor sounds funny, I think it's because the sounds she's trying to make are hard for her."

"Let's look at the script," said Paul. "Let's see. She's the lookout, right? She spies a ship." He flipped through the pages. "Here it is." He showed the script to Robert.

Robert read Taylor's lines. "'Ahoy, mates! There's a ship on the horizon!' Remember?"

"Yeah. So what?"

"So, the 'Ahoy, mates' part was okay, but the next part sounded funny. That's because there was a *th* and an *sh* in those lines." Robert made faces as he exaggerated those sounds.

He got up from the computer. "What do you think it's like, not being able to hear?" He covered his ears.

"It sounds like . . . well . . . quiet," said Paul.

Robert laughed, but he said, "I'm serious. Think about it." He covered his ears.

Paul covered his ears, too.

"Can you hear me?" asked Robert.

"Yeah, a little," said Paul. "Can you hear me?"

Robert nodded. "Yeah, I could hear you, just not as good."

Robert pulled a tissue out of a box near Paul's bed and ripped it in half. He made two balls out of the torn tissue and stuffed them in his ears.

"Go ahead, talk."

Paul started. "I don't really know what to say, but I'm saying it, anyway. Blah-blah-blah."

Robert took out the earplugs. "You said 'I don't really know what to say, but I'm saying it, anyway. Blah-blah-blah.' But it sounded all muffled."

"Hmmm. I wonder if that's how Taylor hears," said Paul.

"That's what I was wondering, too," said Robert. He took out the earplugs and dropped them in the wastebasket.

Robert couldn't imagine what it must be like to hear nothing at all.

Invitations

When Robert sat in his seat at Table Four the next morning, some of the girls were in a cluster by the reading table, buzzing about something.

"What's up?" he asked Vanessa.

"Susanne Lee is having a birthday party."

"Oh." Parties didn't interest Robert, especially parties with girls. He took his notebook and a pencil out of his backpack.

Taylor was looking his way. Robert realized he wasn't looking directly at her when he spoke, so she probably couldn't understand what he said.

"We're talking about Susanne Lee. She's going to have a party." He made sure Taylor could read his lips.

She nodded that she understood.

Mrs. Bernthal asked the class to settle down. "We're having a spelling test today, remember? Let's do it and get it over with," she said.

They groaned, but took out their pencils while Pamela Rose handed out paper.

Robert got the first few words right, but when Mrs. Bernthal gave them the word *afraid*, he froze. He never could remember if it was spelled with an "ai" or an "ia." He picked the "ia." That made him nervous about the next few words. When he handed his paper in, he wasn't at all sure how he did.

It was almost a relief when they read their reports on rain forests. He knew he did a good job on that. He had spent a lot of time on a diorama, putting monkeys in trees and all. And it was the first time ever that he had read two books for one report.

At lunchtime, the girls were buzzing again. The word got around to Robert and Paul. Susanne Lee's parents told her she could invite twelve friends to her party. It was going to be at The Pirate's Cove, a neat restaurant where they handed out cardboard pirate hats and swords to kids and gave them their meals in cardboard treasure chests.

Robert felt a pang of jealousy. There were twenty kids in the class—no, twenty-one now, with Taylor. He didn't think he would be one of the kids invited, but he really liked those hats and swords.

"So who do you think is going?" Robert asked Paul.

Paul had a mouthful of sandwich, so he just shrugged. After he swallowed, he said, "I don't know. Who do you think?"

"I guess it's just girls," said Robert, trying not to think about those hats and swords.

"Yeah," said Paul, taking another bite of his sandwich.

Outside on the playground, Robert and Paul were horsing around when Brian blurted out to Kevin that he had been invited, and Kevin said he was, too. Susanne Lee had not handed out all the invitations yet. It was funny. Not everyone liked Susanne Lee, but everyone wanted to go to her party.

It was pretty clear by the time lunch period was over that the kids who hadn't received an invitation yet were feeling bad. They seemed to cluster together, except for Taylor, who was by herself.

Robert felt squirmy. He didn't know why it bothered him. Sometimes when they chose sides for teams nobody picked him, and he didn't feel bad like he did now. For one thing, he knew he wasn't very good at sports. And he always ended up on a team—that was the rule. Nobody got left out.

He looked at Paul. Paul wasn't invited, either, but it didn't seem to bother Paul at all. Robert wished he could be that cool.

In the classroom, after lunch, they had to do pages in their math workbooks. Robert looked over at Susanne Lee. She was writing in her workbook. She probably knew all the answers. He never saw her erase anything.

He imagined a giant pencil eraser coming down and wiping Susanne Lee right out of her seat.

Lester's Announcement

Lester barreled into the classroom the next morning, ready to burst.

"I found it! I found it!" he cried.

Everyone looked at him.

"Found what?" asked Emily.

"Robert's bicycle! I found it yesterday when I made the rounds with my dad picking up trash."

The children gathered around as Lester continued. Even Mrs. Bernthal was fascinated. Robert was so stunned he didn't know what to say. Even the police weren't sure they'd find the bike.

"We stopped at this house, and I saw a bike leaning against a gate. It looked suspicious. The handlebars were backwards and the fenders were gone. But it still looked like that bike in the picture Paul drew."

Lester pulled the paper out of his pocket as he caught his breath. It was all folded and wrinkled, like someone had really been using it.

"Then what?" asked Joey.

"A little kid came over while I was looking at it and asked me what my problem was. I told him my problem was that the bike was stolen. The kid looked scared when I said that. 'It's my brother's!' he shouted. 'Go get your brother,' I said. 'We'll see about that.' The kid ran away and didn't come back."

"Lester, that is amazing," said Mrs. Bernthal. "But are you sure it's the bike you were looking for?"

"Yeah, I'm sure."

"When can I get it?" asked Robert. He felt a rush of excitement at the thought of seeing his bike again.

"Wait till I fix it up," said Lester. "You can't ride it the way it is."

"Great," said Robert. "How long will it take?"

"My mom says I have to do my schoolwork first." Lester shrugged. "And I have to learn my lines and paint the sets."

Robert hardly had a chance to be disappointed.

"We'll help you," said Lucy Ritts. "Come on. We'll go over your lines right now."

"And Taylor is helping us paint," said Robert, "so we'll get the backdrop done. Right, Paul?"

Paul nodded.

"Okay." Lester found his script and went off with Lucy to the Reading Table.

Mrs. Bernthal smiled. "You almost don't need me anymore," she said.

Meanwhile, Susanne Lee went around the room handing out the rest of her party invitations. Jesse Meiner got one, then Abby Ranko and Melissa Thurm.

Robert felt his stomach churn as Susanne Lee came over to Table Four. She handed one to Vanessa, then stopped next to Paul and put an invitation in front of him. It seemed like a long time before she put one down in front of Robert, too.

It was a relief, but Robert looked at Taylor. Even though there were four of them sitting at Table Four, Taylor looked all alone.

He wished he hadn't been given an invitation. It felt wrong. Why didn't he say something to Susanne Lee? Didn't she know she was being obnoxious, making people feel left out?

As they were painting away on the painter's cloth that afternoon, Robert looked at Taylor's work. She had painted the wood on the ship to look just like real wood.

"How did you do that?" he said. "That's really good."

There was no response. Taylor was working away with her brush.

Robert tapped her gently on the shoulder. When she looked up, he said again, "How did you do that? It's really good."

Taylor smiled and said, "Thank you," in that heavy-sounding way. Robert realized this time it was the sound that caused it. She also touched her lips with her free hand, then moved her hand forward with the palm up.

That was the first time she used sign language with him, and he understood immediately that it meant "thank you." He gave her a thumbs-up. Hmmm. Maybe that was sign language, too.

Rehearsing

"**R**un!" shouted Mrs. Bernthal. Melissa was looking left and right. "Left! Stage left!" called Mrs. Bernthal. Melissa ran, first one way, then the other.

"Melissa, you must pick up your cue on time," said Mrs. Bernthal. "When you hear Robert—I mean Dirty Pete—shout 'Get out of me way!' you run for your life. Quickly! And exit stage left."

Robert felt sorry for Melissa. The lefts and rights were really confusing. They were using the stage at the far end of the

Community Room. Mrs. Bernthal had taught them that stage left was the part of the stage on the actor's left as he faced the audience, but it was hard to remember that when you were up there onstage, and there were two doors, one on each side.

Even though he knew it was confusing for Melissa, Robert felt good, too, that he had done such a good job spooking her. As the grimy pirate, Dirty Pete, he had made himself as fierce as he could, with a black mustache and a patch over one eye, and had jumped out at her as he shouted his line. That's probably what made her miss her cue.

Yeah, he was a pretty good pirate, if he did say so himself. Maybe he should think about being an actor someday.

They had spent all afternoon rehearsing the play. In only three days, they would perform it for their parents as well as other classes. Some kids still didn't know their lines. The costumes weren't all ready because Emily's mother had run out of fabric for the sailors' outfits.

There were still no pirate hats, and the sword for the pirate captain was too sharp to use. Brian was supposed to make a wooden one covered with aluminum foil, but Brian was out with a cold, and nobody knew if he'd be back in time to bring the sword or even be in the play. Jesse Meiner had to learn his lines as well as his own so he could take Brian's part if he was out sick.

Robert didn't know how they'd ever be able to do a dress rehearsal or be ready in time for Friday night's performance.

On Friday morning, Taylor came in with a big grin on her face. Robert didn't remember seeing her that happy before. It couldn't be just the play.

He looked in her face. "What are you so happy about?"

Taylor pulled back her hair, and there was a bright red hearing aid wrapped around her ear. She pulled back the hair on the other side. There was one there, too.

"Cool," said Robert. "Can you really hear better now?"

Taylor nodded.

"No more signing?" Robert found he was a little disappointed. He liked learning sign language.

"Say something," Taylor said, and she turned away from him.

"Hello, Taylor, how are you today, and aren't your hearing aids bee-yoo-tee-ful?" said Robert.

Taylor turned around, laughing. "I am fine. And yes, they are bee-yoo-tee-ful," she said.

"That's great!" said Robert.

"I'm still learning to sign, because the hearing aids could break or get lost. Or my hearing may get worse." She didn't even look sad when she said that. It seemed like she just knew it was possible, and that was that. "I have to go for speech therapy," she continued, "to learn to make all my sounds correctly. I couldn't do it until I could hear the sounds clearly."

So that's what it was! Taylor couldn't hear sounds a hundred percent, so she couldn't say them a hundred percent.

"Hey look, everybody," Robert called. "Taylor's got neat new hearing aids."

The kids all came over to see.

"Cool," said Kevin Kransky.

"They're awesome," said Elizabeth.

"I love the color," said Pamela.

Taylor looked like she was really happy.

"All right, everyone," Mrs. Bernthal said. There's a dress rehearsal today. Don't forget."

They had been asked to stay after school for the rehearsal, so parents would be picking them up at 4:30 today. The school buses would be long gone by then. Robert's dad was going to come for him and Paul.

"And the performance is tonight at eight o'clock," said Mrs. Bernthal. "You must all be here by seven o'clock to get into your makeup and costumes."

Ms. Valentine came rushing in with a shopping bag. "Here are your pirate hats," she said. "I'm sorry they're so late, but they got wet, and the paint ran, so I had to do them all over again. I had the fifth grade help me during their art class. Otherwise I wouldn't have had them here on time."

The best hat of all was Lester's. He was playing the part of the Pirate King. The hat was black with a white skull and cross-bones painted on the front. When Lester put the hat on his head, he really looked like the king of the pirates.

They got through the dress rehearsal with only a few mistakes. One was that Lester forgot his lines.

"Lester, I thought you had your lines memorized better than that," said Mrs. Bernthal.

"I . . . I did," Lester stammered. "I don't know what happened."

"Don't let your costume go to your head. Practice a couple more times with someone before the performance. You can't forget your lines tonight. Everyone is counting on you."

"Okay," said Lester, quieter than usual.

At the last minute, just as they were about to go home for the day, one of the cardboard waves keeled over, and Paul had to fuss with it and use a lot of duct tape to get it to stand upright.

Riding home with his dad and Paul, Robert wished the car would just keep on going, faster and faster, to anywhere. It's not that he didn't want to do the play; he was just so excited. He didn't want this day to be over, ever. He was having much too much fun being Dirty Pete with the smelly feet.

Stage Fright

"**R**ob! Yo, Rob!"

Robert whirled around. Lester was trying to make his way through the crowd of pirates and sailors backstage to get to him.

"Hi!" said Lester in a robust voice, when he reached Robert.

"Hi," said Robert, as he glued his mustache down with spirit gum. His dad gave him the spirit gum from his collection of horror stuff that he dressed up in every Halloween. "What's up?"

"My mom is here!"

"That's great." Robert checked the mustache in a pocket mirror Mrs. Bernthal handed him.

"She never came to anything before," Lester added.

Robert stopped fussing with the mustache and looked at Lester. He didn't know what to say. His mom and dad had come to everything Robert was ever in. Paul's parents did, too, sometimes with little Nick.

"You'll be great!" said Robert. "You're a terrific Pirate King. Wait till she sees you!"

The audience grew quiet as Susanne Lee took her cue from Mrs. Bernthal. There was no curtain, so she just walked out on the stage while the rest of them stayed out of sight behind the entrance door on the stage.

"Welcome to Clover Hill Elementary School," said Susanne Lee. "Tonight the children of Mrs. Bernthal's class will perform *The Secret of the Pirate King*, by Lenore Stanley. We hope you will enjoy it. Oh, and please turn off your cell phones at this time. Thank you." She said it all perfectly.

Backstage, Mrs. Bernthal was trying to keep the noise down. "Ready, children?"

They nodded. They were ready. Except for Lester. Lester looked like he was going to barf.

"Lester, are you okay?" asked Mrs. Bernthal.

Lester shook his head.

"What's the matter? You know your lines, don't you?"

Lester nodded, but he looked kind of green.

Mrs. Bernthal went over to him. She took his hand. "It's okay, Lester," she said. "Anyone can have stage fright. Some of the best actors do."

Lester was listening, but he looked scared out of his mind.

Robert wished he could do something. He knew once Lester got onstage he'd be fine. But right now, he was a mess.

"Take deep breaths," Mrs. Bernthal said, still holding Lester's hand. "Deep breaths," she said. "Take deep breaths, Lester."

Robert saw the Pirate King's hat on the floor next to Lester and picked it up. He came around and put it on Lester's head.

"Look-it here, mates," said Robert, to the other kids. "It's our Pirate King. Three cheers for our king." The kids sent up a cheer. Lester smiled. He stood up.

"I'm okay," he said, even if he still looked shaky. He took his place by the stage door.

Mrs. Bernthal looked relieved. "Thank you, Robert. And thank you, Lester." She opened the door.

Two of the pirates walked out, one with a kerchief around his head and the other with a fake knife between his teeth. They carried coils of rope that they dropped near the front of the stage. Lester came out and called to the pirates in a booming voice. "Come here, you scrungy varlets!"

The play was underway.

The cardboard waves stayed upright for almost the whole performance, and when one of them finally fell over, the actors stepped over it until it was cleared away. And when one of the backdrops caught a breeze and swayed against the back wall, someone ad-libbed, "Storm at sea!" and everyone in the audience and in the play laughed and applauded.

At the end, the audience gave the cast a hearty round of applause. Paul got a special round for his amazing set and he, in turn, thanked his team—Lester, Robert,

Taylor, and Lucy—for helping. Mrs.
Bernthal thanked each of the committees,
and the parents who pitched in to help
with props, costumes, sets, chauffeuring,
and labor.

"Thank you so much for coming," said
Mrs. Bernthal. "There are refreshments

across the hall in the lobby. Please meet us there, where the cast and crew will join you."

People started streaming out of the Community Room toward the refreshment tables. Robert hurried along behind them.

He watched as Lester tried making his way, too, but kept getting stopped by parents who told him how terrific he was. Some took his picture. By the time Lester found his mom, he was grinning from ear to ear. So was she.

Proof

"Charlie, you really missed an excellent performance last night," said Mrs. Dorfman to Robert's older brother. She placed the box from Pete's Pizza Palace on the coffee table next to the paper plates and napkins. Pizza and movies were usually on Fridays, but this week, because of Robert's play, they were moved to Saturday.

"Yeah, I know," said Charlie, grabbing the first slice. "Dirty Pete with the smelly feet." Huckleberry stood there, wagging his tail and waiting.

Robert's dad teased, too. "We were thinking that Robert might have a career as a pirate someday if we lived in different times."

Robert didn't mind the teasing. He was still flying high from last night. He helped himself to a slice of pizza and put one aside for Huckleberry, to cool off.

"What are we watching?" asked Charlie, looking through the DVDs on the coffee table.

"*Lord of the Rings!*" cried Robert. "Please, please, please. . . ."

"I think we can accommodate Dirty Pete," said his dad. "What do you think?"

"Sure," said Charlie, planting himself in his favorite place on the couch.

Robert settled on the floor with his legs crossed, Huckleberry right next to him.

Robert took the cooled pizza slice, tore it up, and put the pieces on a paper plate for Huck, who happily scarfed them down.

Robert's mom put the disk in the DVD player, and Charlie grabbed for the remote. Just as the FBI warning came on about copying the disk, the doorbell rang.

"Hey, it's the FBI," said Charlie.

Robert laughed as his mom went to the door.

"Robert," she called a moment later. "It's Lester. For you."

Robert got up, and Huckleberry trailed after him. Lester was at the door, all right, and he had a bicycle with him.

"Yo, Rob," said Lester. "I thought you might like your bike."

"Wow. Yeah," said Robert. He stared at the bike. It looked different.

"Come in, Lester," said Robert's mom. "We're having pizza. Would you like to join us?"

"Um . . . no thanks, Mrs. D. I have to go. My dad is waiting in the truck." He pointed out to the street. I just wanted to drop this off."

Lester looked at Robert. "It looks different because there are no fenders. The seat was too high, so I fixed that, and I turned the handlebars back to the way they were before."

"Lester, you fixed it yourself?" said Robert's mom.

"Yeah," said Lester. "I looked at some old bikes in the junkyard, but I couldn't find the right fenders."

Robert stared at the bike.

"Robert, aren't you going to thank Lester?" his mom asked.

"Huh? Oh, yeah. Thanks, Lester." He took the bike from Lester. He rolled it back and forth. It felt okay. "It's a great bike," said Lester. "You can ride it without fenders, but you may want to get a new reflector light for the back of your seat."

Robert didn't know what else to say except "thank you." Was it his bike, or was it swiped from someone else? He was still wondering, but he had to say something.

"This is really great." He smiled, because his mom was watching and he knew he should. "So I guess I'll see you in school Monday, right?"

"Right," said Lester. He grinned. "You're welcome. I'm glad I had that description of your bike."

"Yeah," said Robert. But half the things in that description were no longer on the bike. How could Lester be so sure?

After Lester left, Robert settled down again and got lost in the movie, but when it was over and he got up, he saw the bike leaning up against the wall near the front door.

How could he find out if Lester had brought him the right bicycle?

He called Paul and told him about the bike and his doubts.

"Well, ride it," said Paul.

"What do you mean?" said Robert.

"Just get on the bike and really ride it.

You'll know your own bike once you do that."

Was that true? Robert had to give it a try.

"Okay. It's too late tonight, but do you want to go over to Van Saun Park in the morning?"

"Sure," said Paul. "I'll be at your house at nine o'clock."

Surprise Party

As they sailed along toward Van Saun Park, Robert stood up on the pedals and shouted.

"Wheeeeeeeee!"

Paul rode right behind him.

Whooping his way down the street, Robert felt the pedals under his feet and the grips in his hands. The seat might be slightly high, but it was his seat.

It was just like Paul promised. Once Robert got on his bike and rode it, he knew it was his.

That Lester was something. Robert was so afraid Lester had captured the wrong bike that he didn't thank him the way he should have.

"You just thought he was taking his Pirate King role too seriously," said Paul, when Robert told him what he had been thinking.

"That's it! I thought he was being a pirate, taking what he wanted for his own good."

"Maybe YOU are the one who's taking the pirate play too seriously," said Paul, laughing.

Robert laughed. He had to agree.

They stopped by the duck pond and laid their bikes down in the grass and sat down next to them to watch the ducks.

After a few moments just staring at the ducks, Robert blurted out, "I'm not going to Susanne Lee's party."

Paul turned to him, looking surprised.
"How come?"

"Well, remember how it felt all that time
while we waited to be invited?"

"Yeah. It felt terrible. But I thought you
wanted to go."

"I did. I wanted to be invited like everybody else. But when I looked at Taylor I couldn't help thinking how bad she must have felt. And the other kids, too, like Lester."

"You're worried about Lester?"

"Well, you know what I mean."

"Yeah," said Paul, smiling. "He was a really great Pirate King, wasn't he?"

Robert nodded. "Everybody loved him."

There was a long silence.

"We should have our own party," said Robert.

"Susanne Lee will have a fit," Paul said. "Where?"

"My house. Your house. Wait, I know! How about Van Saun Park?" Robert felt the excitement rising.

"What a cool idea!" said Paul. "Now Susanne Lee will REALLY have a fit. A double fit."

74

"We can ride over on our bikes," said Robert.

"We'll have to call everyone who didn't get an invitation to Susanne Lee's party."

"Yeah. Let's go."

They picked up their bikes and pedaled off to make phone calls.

The first one was to Susanne Lee, to tell her he and Paul could not come to her party. She had a fit, just as they had predicted. And when they told her they were going to a party of their own, Paul was right. She had a double fit.

Good Signs

Susanne Lee pranced up to Table Four on Monday. She looked right past Taylor at Robert.

"Robert, and you, too, Paul," she said. "I think you're mean. I'm sorry I invited you in the first place." She bounced back to her table.

Robert looked at Taylor. With her hearing aids, she must have heard Susanne Lee clearly. She seemed to be writing something in her notebook, but Robert noticed her hand didn't move across the page. She looked up out of the corner of her eye and smiled at him.

Over the weekend, Paul and Robert told their moms about their idea, and Paul's mom said she would make them brownies for their party, and some lemonade. Robert's mom bought them paper plates, cups, and napkins. Even Lester's mom wanted to help when she heard about it, and said she would send some cookies over with Lester on Saturday.

This morning, they gave paper invitations made by Paul to all the kids not going to Susanne Lee's party. The invitations read:

COME TO A GREAT PARTY
AT VAN SAUN PARK
NEXT SATURDAY
12 O'CLOCK NOON
P.S. EVERYONE IS WELCOME!

At the bottom was a picture of kids playing. Some of them were on bikes. An arrow pointed to one of the boys on a bike. ROBERT, it said by the arrow. Another arrow pointed to the bike. ROBERT'S BIKE, it read.

The kids loved it.

The best part was the Van Saun Park kids now had something to talk about when the other kids buzzed about Susanne Lee's party. Vanessa told Robert her mom and Susanne Lee's mom were friends, otherwise she would have come to their party.

When Susanne Lee passed Robert at the pencil sharpener, she said, "You're ruining my party!"

"I only invited people you didn't," said Robert, checking his pencil point.

Susanne Lee looked like she would explode. Her face got very red. "I could only invite twelve people," she cried. "What was I supposed to do?"

"I don't know," said Robert. "But you didn't have to make everyone else feel bad."

Susanne Lee had nothing to say to that. She turned quickly and walked away.

"Uh-oh," said Paul.

"Well, it's not my fault," said Robert.

Mrs. Bernthal brought the class to attention.

"Boys and girls, I have good news. On Monday, we're going to start learning to sign. We'll learn American Sign Language. We have Taylor to thank for bringing this to our attention. I think you will find it fascinating."

She made the same "thank you" sign Robert remembered getting from Taylor,

by touching her lips with her hand, then moving her hand forward with the palm up. Taylor blushed, but Robert knew she must be happy.

"And now, let's see how our story ends." Mrs. Bernthal picked up *The Tale of Despereaux* and started to read.

It ends happily, Robert said to himself. *All good stories have happy endings.*

BARBARA SEULING is a well-known author of fiction and nonfiction books for children, including many books about Robert. She divides her time between New York City and Vermont.

PAUL BREWER lives in San Diego, California, with his wife and two daughters. He is the author and illustrator of *You Must Be Joking!*